To.

Best Wishes
and
Aloha!
2 Lt Monica Conter Benning ANC

A Real Nurse's Dream

Monica Conter Benning

Written in March/April 1943 ~ Apalachicola, Florida

Compiled and Published in June, 2008 ~ Fort Myers, Florida

Books Highlighting the Life of Lieutenant Monica Conter Benning ANC

1   "None More Courageous" by Stewart H. Hollbrook
     Published - The Macmillan Company - New York - Copyright 1942
     Chapter 14 - Young Women At War - Pages 171-172-173

2.   "Nurses in Action" by Colonel Julia O. Flikke AUS
     Publisher - JB Lippincott Company - New York - Copyright 1943
     Part V - First Blood - Page 163

3.   "Day of Infamy" by Walter Lord
     Publisher - Henry Holt and Company - New York - Copyright 1957
     Chapter 1 -Isn't that a Beautiful Sight - Pages 3-4-10-59-149-210

4.   Smithsonian Magazine 12-91, Page 78, Chapter 1, Paragraph 7, Famous writer William
     Zinsser when visiting Pearl Harbor included in his current article, a lengthy and quoted
     paragraph from Walter Lord's best seller "Day of Infamy" which begins, Monica Conter,
     a young Army nurse and...

5.   "We're In This War Too" by Judy Barrett Litoff and David C. Smith
     Publisher - Oxford University Press - New York - Copyright 1994
     Pages 17-18-19-51

6.   "Pearl Harbor The Movie and The Moment"
     Published by HYPERION - New York - Text copyright © 2001
     Disney Enterprises Ltd. Produced by Newmarket
     Chapter-The Nurses at Pearl Harbor Page 44

7.   "What Made Us Who We Are Today" by Mary Timpe Robsman
     Publisher - Terra Sancta Press, Inc. - Melbourne, Fl. Copyright 2002
     Eyewitness to History - Monica Conter Benning Pages (9-10) 11-12-13

8.   "Slice of Life" Fifteen True Stories by Members of The Landings Writers Club
     in Fort Myers, Fl.
     Published by 48 Hr Books Copyright 2006 by The Landings Writers Club
     Chapter - The Healing Tree by Monica Conter Benning

9.   "A Real Nurse's Dream" by Monica Conter Benning
     Publisher - 48 hr Books - Copyright © 2007 by Monica Conter Benning
     Written in 1943 at the request of Col. Julia O. Flikke, Supt. of ANC. She
     Suggested my 3-year ANC career include the offical ANC recruiting model nurse with
     her, experience during the Japanese horrific attack 12-07-41, my romance/wedding with
     Barney and flight from Hickam to Washington D.C. with Capt. Eddie Rickenbacker.

ISBN 978-1-59916-183-9

Dedication

This publication is dedicated to the following Regular Army Nurses, with whom I worked, untiringly, on that fateful Sunday, December 7, 1941 at Station Hospital, Hickam Field, Oahu T.H.:

First Lieutenant Annie Fox,
Second Lieutenants Irene Boyd*, Kathleen Coberly, Sarah Entrikin,
and Winifred Mallett.

* There were only two Army Nurses at Hickam Field hospital on duty at 7:55 AM, December 7, 1941 — Irene Boyd and myself, Monica Conter.

Acknowledgement

"The story is a real nurse's dream, and every young nurse in the country will love to read it"!

- Alexander Key, 1943

The Apalachicola Times, pg. 4, on August 23, 1979:

Alexander Key Dies at 71 - Alexander Key, a nationally known author, artist and former resident of Apalachicola, Florida, died July 25, 1979 in Eufala, Alabama, at the age of 71. Originally from Quincy, FL, Key moved to Apalachicola in 1936 and left for World War II during the early 1940's.

Two of his novels, *Island Light* and *The Wrath and the Wind*, were centered in Apalachicola and the old town of St. Joseph. Numerous short stories and articles, including many that appeared in the old Saturday Evening Post, were also featured in this geographical area. Of special interest, his novel, *Return to Witch Mountain*, was recently made into a Disney movie of the same name.

An outstanding artist, Key illustrated many of his books with black and white drawings, the originals of which have become valued by art collectors.

Appreciation

I would like to give special appreciation to the following individuals for their expertise, guidance, encouragement, time and editing abilities to make this publication a final reality for others to read.

Ruth M. Anderson, BSN, MSN, Lt. Col., USAF, NC (Ret.),
Edna Elizabeth Domino, BSN, MSN, ARNP-C, Major, USAF, NC (Ret.),
John Michael Domino, Ed. D., Major, USAF (Ret.), and
Wanda L. Jacobs

Foreword

I wrote this true story in the months of March and April 1943 — while sitting in my parent's home, in the front bedroom at 96 Fifth Street, Apalachicola, Florida. This was written at the request of Colonel Julia O. Flikke, Superintendent of the Army Nurse Corps, Office of the Surgeon General, Washington, D.C.

It was during the final days of my three-year, U.S. Army Nurse Corps commitment that I found myself back in Washington D.C. I was there December 19 through 21, 1942, where a special, modified B-24 flight from Hickam Field, Hawaii to Bolling Field, D.C. had ended. Captain Eddie Rickenbacker — you may remember his airplane crash in the Pacific where he and his crew spent 21 days on a raft, had personally arranged to include me on that flight so I could be the assigned nurse-attendant aboard.

During lunch, as a guest of Colonel Flikke, she requested that I write a personal history of my three years in the Army Nurse Corps. This account was to entail a time during 1940 and early 1941, when I was recognized as the official "recruiting model." With her, we vied for the Red Cross Registered Nurses to join the Army Nurse Corps. In addition to this tribute, I was asked to detail my experiences of the Japanese attack on December 7, 1941 and thereafter. In order to sense the events of that time, Colonel Flikke asked me to include the story of my romance and marriage to Lt. Bernard (Barney) F. Benning, now Lt. Col. AUS Reserve Retired. Finally, I was asked to portray the events of my trip to the mainland with Captain Eddie Rickenbacker.

By the time the story was completed and sent to Colonel Flikke, she had retired due to physical disability. The manuscript was eventually returned to me and was never used nor published, until now.

-Monica Conter Benning, 2007

***

The following story is a true account of the many exciting and unusual experiences that I had during the happiest three years of my life — the three years I was on active duty as a Second Lieutenant in the Regular Army Nurse Corps.

-Monica Conter Benning, 1943

In the small, historic and unique town of Apalachicola, Florida—a population of 3500, nothing exciting ever happened to break the monotony of one's existence. Most lived a slow, easy, happy-go-lucky life, taking all small occurrences in their daily stride. Weddings, funerals and fires occasionally gave cause for the entire town to "turn out" en masse. Pleasure was limited to weddings, bridge and beach parties, dances, school festivities and movies. In this quaint little village I passed the first years of my life—all in a quiet atmosphere and was graduated from High School in May 1931. My family consisted of my father, Augustus Eugene Conter, MD; my mother, Mary Ann (Mamie) Lichtenfelt; my brother Charles and sister, Alice Maria—also known as Doll, her nickname.

I entered Providence Hospital's School of Nursing, Mobile, Alabama in May 1936. While there, including Spring Hill College, I started a three-year course that was rather uneventful with the exception of achieving a few outstanding honors: one of four members in the choir and an honor's student of my graduating class (which was one of the highest scores in the State Board Examination at that time). I was also the only member of my class offered a position as Head Nurse of the Obstetrical Department, in my Alma Mater.

In September 1939, I passed the Public Health Civil Service Examination in nursing. Then on November 13, I was offered and accepted a position at the U.S. Marine Hospital in Baltimore, Maryland. Baltimore however, sounded like the North Pole! As such, I immediately went to a department store and bought a muskrat fur coat for $75.00, putting ten dollars down, and paying ten dollars a month. (My parents stored it when I went overseas.) After several weeks on duty in Maryland, a nurse friend of mine said to me, "Why aren't you an Army Nurse? Surely you could qualify. It offers so much—a relative rank of Lieutenant, a good salary, nice working hours and Foreign Service. Why, you could travel to Hawaii or the Philippines if you wanted." The idea of traveling appealed to me most of all, however, I told her I didn't think I could qualify because I hadn't much experience, having finished nursing school less than a year ago. Then she looked up at me and exclaimed, "Well, I bet you could be accepted in the Army Nurse Corps. I was rejected because of my height. I was too short!"

Shortly after that experience, things really began to happen. The exact same evening while looking over the new monthly issue of the American Journal of Nursing, I saw an article stating that the Army Nurse Corps was expanding. They were offering immediate appointments to any Red Cross graduate nurse who fully qualified. Having acquainted myself with the requirements, I immediately went to Washington D.C. My intentions were to have an interview with Major Julia O. Flikke (who was later in my career promoted to Colonel and to Chief Superintendent of the Army Nurse Corps). The Superintendent of the Army Nurse Corps always had her office in connection with the Surgeon General's Office of the United States Army. When I arrived, I was exceedingly impressed by her poise and her quiet understanding manner. She made me feel as if the Army Nurse Corps could not get along without me. Her staff was equally gracious. Consequently, it took little or no persuasion for me to realize the Army was my future career as it offered everything I desired.

In less than a month, on January 19, 1940, I was sworn in as a Regular Army Nurse. I was given the relative rank of Second Lieutenant and assigned to Walter Reed General Hospital, Army Medical Center in Washington, D.C.

At first, it was hard to realize that here I was, living in the Nation's Capitol, the very hub—the pulse of this country's political activity. Right under my nose was all of the advantages and pleasures for which I had always longed. There were but a few concerts given by famous pianists, singers, or symphony orchestras at the Constitution Hall that I did not attend. The same was for the wonderful stage plays at the National Theater. At that time, my favorites were Alfred Lunt and Lynn Fontaine in "There Shall Be No Night," and in concert, Jeanette MacDonald and Nelson Eddie.

In my enthusiasm, I made several trips to Baltimore to attend the Metropolitan Opera, Ballet Russe de Monte Carlo and even the Preakness horse race on May 30—the very day "Bimelech" won first place!

The city of Washington itself held my attention with its beautiful buildings—both new and historical, as well as its parks, museums and art galleries. The scenic drives, Mt. Vernon, the Skyline and others, all in short distance from this place I now called "home." My love of the city was also in part for the merry and lighter side—the excellent movies and shows, the hotels with their beautiful cocktail lounges, the large stores with lovely clothes, and my weakness—the excellent restaurants. My favorite was "The Troika," in Russian, meaning SLED. I also took advantage of the area and visited near-by cities like Philadelphia, Richmond, and

New York. To me, this was an education in itself. As you might surmise, by the end of each month, I was financially "broke," however, I can never recall regretting any of my "escapades."

Occasionally, we had formals at the Nurses Quarters, which were always most enjoyable. It was a real pleasure to have a dinner guest just to "show off" our lovely Delano Hall—our home.

CONTER HOUSE OPENS AS ART CENTER IN APALACHICOLA

11/2/2006

The Board of the Historic Apalachicola Foundation, Inc. is pleased to announce the opening of the 1845 Fry Conter House on November 25, 2006 as a center for the arts. The House is located at 96 Fifth Street in historic Apalachicola. The Secretary of State's Division of Historical Resources assisted the Foundation in the restoration of the historic building, as did many other private and public entities.

Conter House – c.1845

John Gorrie (1803-1855)

Colonel Flikke requested my story and I wrote it in 1943

Walter Reed General Hospital – Jan.1940

Cover & inside photo of
Nurses in Uniform, Red Cross Courier,
"Uncle Sam Needs Nurses"
L-R Margaret Swan,
Helen Meikle, Monica Conter

Preakness Race, (Bimelech won 1st)
& Photo taken same day 5/1940

Graduation –Providence Hospital
5/1939 (M.Conter, 6th from left)

In the fall of 1940, after spending two weeks "leave" with my parents in Florida, I returned to Washington and learned that the Army was going to call Red Cross Reserve Nurses to active-duty. One day the telephone rang in my room — it was our Chief Nurse advising, "Major Flikke would like for you to represent the Army Nurse Corps (ANC) when the first Red Cross Reserve Nurse, Agnes Rosele, is sworn in to active-duty. This will take place tomorrow, October 10, 1940, at the Red Cross National Headquarters. Wear your white uniform, OD (Olive Drab) cap and cape as some national press representatives and official photographers will be there. Major Flikke will call for you at 0800." Well, you can imagine my excitement at being selected out of all the nurses in the Army to represent this great organization! Not to mention my picture appearing with Major Flikke in newspapers all over the country!

This was indeed the beginning of what might be termed a "publicity career" for me as an Army Nurse. In a few days, Harris and Ewing, one of the large photo studios, telephoned and requested to have my picture on file. This same studio was well known for keeping photos on file of many famous celebrities nationwide. Naturally, I felt very honored and thrilled with it all.

In December that same year, I was again called upon to represent the ANC. This time a color photo was developed for use by the Red Cross Nursing Service in a recruiting booklet titled, "Uncle Sam Needs Nurses." I posed with a Navy Nurse, Margaret Swann, and a Red Cross Nurse, Helen Meikle. Thousands of these booklets were released and distributed nationwide. Naturally, I kept one!

When I returned from my Christmas leave in Florida that year, I received the most beautiful gardenia corsage I had ever seen. It was from Miss Mary Beard, the National Director of the Red Cross Nursing Service. I wish there had been some way to preserve it, however, I still have the greeting card that came with it, of which I indeed treasure.

Here, I would like to mention how happy I was to be able to attend the Inaugural Gala (Concert) and the Inauguration of President Roosevelt. Although I am an "Independent" voter, I still consider this one of the outstanding moments of my life!

On March 11, 1941, I had the honor of being on the Jane Delano Memorial program held at the Red Cross National Headquarters. There were five of us who spoke on the radio, Mutual Broadcasting—providing coast-to-coast "hook-up" that morning, for purposes of recruiting Army and Navy nurses. Attending were Major Julia O. Flikke, Miss Sue S. Dauser, (Superintendent of the Navy Nurse Corps), Miss Mary Beard, the announcer and myself. It was such an exciting experience. During this service, a Navy Nurse, Margaret Swann, and I acted as escorts for a Red Cross Nurse, Leone Hawks, who placed a wreath at the foot of the Jane Delano Memorial. Pictures of this event appeared in the April 1941 American Journal of Nursing issue.

After the radio program, Major Flikke called me aside and asked if I would be in uniform at the Blue Room of the Mayflower Hotel the following week as "movies were to be made." This was for the Red Cross—a photo was to be used on the magazine cover of the Red Cross Courier, showing all types of uniforms including those worn by Army, Navy and Red Cross Nurses, a Canteen Worker, Braille Teacher and an Ambulance Driver. Oh, what a thrill it was to be in the movies! Finally, the day arrived, I was there, the movie was made, and my, was I scared! A real screen test couldn't have been more exciting. Movietone made the movie and released their film as "Service Styles," which was narrated by Helen Clair. Yes, you bet I saw it more than once. It was fun to see myself on screen, even if it was only for a minute or two. Later on, the same picture showing me saluting was used as a finale in the Red Cross film, "Women in Uniform," while the song, "Angels of Mercy" was sung.

To top everything wonderful that was happening in my life, I was selected as one of twenty Army nurses privileged to attend the White House Garden party given for veterans at Walter Reed General Hospital. All of the nation's greatest personages were present. It was wonderful being just a few feet from the President himself and even getting the chance to talk several minutes with the First Lady, Eleanor. I remember my conversation with a Nebraska Senator and him saying, "I'm the only farmer here," and the chitchat with the First Lady that followed regarding her son in New England and how he admired the Army Nurse Corps.

In the meantime, many of my Army nurse friends had been transferred—some to Hawaii, others to the Philippines, and still others to Puerto Rico. Hawaii was the assignment I wanted more than anything in the world. As a matter of fact, I was becoming more than anxious, even slightly annoyed that I hadn't received orders for "Foreign Service." Then one day in May 1941, while on duty, I had a message to report to Captain Lyda Keener's office, who was the hospital's Chief Nurse. The usual question '…have I done something wrong?' went through my mind. Upon arriving, somewhat hesitantly, I ventured timidly to ask, "You sent for me?" She smiled and said, "Oh yes, I hear you want to go to Hawaii. How soon can you get ready? Your orders just arrived." For a moment I forgot where I was and I started jumping up and down with excitement. The Assistant-Chief Nurse made the comment, "You see Miss Conter, there is a 'Good Angel' after all." I have thought about that expression many times since.

In June 1941, upon returning to Washington after two weeks of leave with my family, I learned that my orders to sail from Brooklyn, New York had been amended. It was rumored that no more transports would go through the Panama Canal. As such, I was to travel "cross-country" by rail and then sail from San Francisco, California to Hawaii.

Within a few days, while waiting for final travel orders, Representative John M. Vorys, of Ohio, declared in a statement to the press that all Army Nurses were neither young nor pretty. He stated that, "…they were a sad, drab, elderly lot, not at all liable to speed recovery"… In response, the daily paper, The Times Herald, got busy and did a beautiful job defending the ANCs with an article and photographs of several nurses. I again was honored to be one of those nurses whose photo was used. I still have that article.

As I was planning for my trip to Hawaii, I learned that two of my Army Nurse friends—M. Kathleen Coberly (who was to be my future maid of honor), and Helene Grazioso had also received orders for Hawaii, so we planned our trip together. By adding a little more to our travel allowance, we were able to reserve a private drawing room on the train from Washington to San Francisco. This included a marvelous one-day stop at the magnificent Grand Canyon. The trip was absolutely wonderful and is indeed a story in itself.

While in San Francisco, I managed to visit a few of the "highlights." These included the Top of the Mark, Roberts at the Beach, the Cliff House, China Town, a three-hour sightseeing tour of the city and also a last minute shopping spree. Some of the time in San Francisco was spent at Fort Mason taking care of final travel papers. While there, I also had a chance to visit with friends stationed at

Letterman General Hospital. This opportunity turned into one of the nicest parts of the trip.

Finally, the big moment arrived—departure for the "Paradise Isle of the Pacific." This was not on an Army transport, but on the beautiful Matson liner, "Mariposa." It so happened that of the 638 passengers, 75 percent were military-service connected, including 28 personnel from the Army Nurse Corps. Our staterooms were given to us alphabetically, and as good fortune would have it, I was assigned a lovely stateroom on "C" deck. Around 5:00PM, as we were ordered to board ship, the music, "Song of the Islands" was heard along with the sight of confetti and streamers everywhere. Beautiful corsages and floral bouquets, many telegrams and special deliveries from our friends bidding us "farewell," was all so exciting.

On that Friday, July 11, 1941, we slowly pulled away from the pier throwing kisses and waving good-bye to the crowd below. As we finally passed under the famous Golden Gate Bridge and out into the great, vast, blue Pacific, my mind began to ponder future events. I wondered what was in store for me, and what I would experience before I would again see that beautiful bridge. Little did I know that I was soon to live through one of the most horrific days of my life!

The trip overseas was one of the most glamorous events of my career. There were the so-called "private socials" all day, along with the ship's usual scheduled entertainment which included horse racing, teas, the game "Keno," movies, bridge tournaments, formal dances, etc. The trip was grand, but the arrival—that was the biggest thrill of all!

We neared the Hawaiian Islands just after dawn. It was such a beautiful sight—a blue-black silhouette against a lighter blue sky with a flickering of light here and there. The sights changed as we approached near Koko Head and Diamond Head. While having breakfast, some local friends adorned with flower leis came excitedly into the dining room. They had ridden out on the tugboat, which checked out the harbor. I just had to go out on deck and see all there was to see. It was such a sight to behold and was it ever breathtaking—there was Honolulu stretching from the mountaintops to the sea, the white sands of Waikiki, rainbows in the sky, planes "buzzing" our ship, and speedboats racing in the water. As we neared the Aloha tower to dock at the pier, native boys swam out to meet us and would dive for coins, as we tossed them into the sea. Slowly, but surely, we neared the dock and soon we heard the lovely sounds of, "Song of the Islands," played by the Royal Hawaiian Band. Numerous friends were there to meet us, each with many leis hung on their arms, waving and bidding us "Aloha." When my attention was called to the "liquid sunshine" –mist- that was actually floating down, well, it was all I could take. It wasn't long before goose pimples came out all over me.

Having docked and been greeted with the customary "leis and kisses," I received orders to report to the Chief Nurse — Captain Edna Rockafellow, at Tripler General Hospital, located on the outskirts of Honolulu. There I learned I was to bivouac, or room with five other nurses at Hickam Field until the new Nurses Quarters at Tripler was completed. This residence was not expected for completion for approximately four months, so until that time, we were to commute, to and from our temporary quarters.

That same day, I had lunch at the famous Royal Hawaiian Hotel with several nurse friends. It was almost impossible to realize that I was actually at Waikiki, the place that I had longed to see. I found Oahu to be all I had ever hoped or dreamed it would be — romantic, beautiful, scenic, and well, just everything! I loved the ever blooming flowers, the ideal climate, the world famous drives, the pali, the old volcanic mountains, the delightful sea and the beautiful moonlit nights. Duty hours were short and we always rested on our "off-duty hours" so we could dine and dance in the evenings. There were many military posts on the Island and there were equally as many Officers Clubs, so one never became bored — monotony was unknown. There were also twenty male officers to each nurse — the telephones never stopped ringing.

For the first few weeks of my stay, nothing unusual happened. Then one day, Lt. Gene Hughes, an officer friend, of one of the nurses called. He asked if I had plans for the upcoming Saturday night. He said if I didn't have other plans, he would like me to meet an acquaintance of his, Lt. Barney Benning, and that he was from the 97th Coast Artillery Anti-Aircraft Division, Fort Kamehaha, and that Barney was a newcomer to the Islands. A party was planned at the Pearl Harbor Officers Club and he asked if I would like to be escorted by Lt. Benning. I said, "Sure, I would love to go." That moment was the beginning of what turned out to be a "True Romance." We went riding, swimming, dancing, and well, just everywhere together. Of course, I dated others — a little competition is always good, but really, I didn't enjoy being with anyone quite as much as I did with this Lt. "Barney."

Am Journal of Nursing,
"Welcome to the Army Nurse Corps."
First Reserve Nurse called to active duty

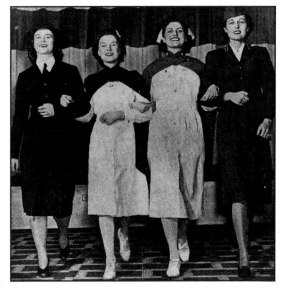

Courier – "Women In Uniform"

 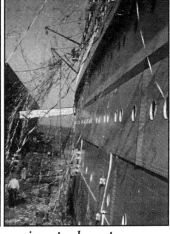

Enroute to San Francisco to depart
on the Mariposa - "Bon Voyage" 7/1941

Monica arrives in Honolulu

First photo taken with Barney,
Ft. "Kam,"–Summer 1941

Hickam Field, Station Hospital 12/41

The new Station Hospital at Hickam Field, which was to be opened in the middle of November 1941, was now nearing completion. I'm sure there wasn't one Army nurse in the Territory of Hawaii who did not want to be assigned there. Only six nurses, however, were to be stationed at this new hospital, including the Chief Nurse. Orders were finally published and my name was included. I was one of those assigned and how happy I was — another time for me to ponder whether this was attributed to "luck" or perhaps "the Good Angel."

One day I received an invitation from one of the pilots who was getting his required "flying hours" completed. This opportunity was a real treat — we flew over beautiful Kauai, the "Garden Island," in a B-17 Flying Fortress. I had hoped my trip would make Barney both envious and jealous. Like all other bachelors, he left numerous women back on the mainland "broken-hearted." "Yes, yes," I would say, "…tell me more," as he talked of other ladies. In spite of his bragging, I knew he was interested in me. I loved his great sense of humor, his politeness, intellect, good looks, and the fact that he had bought a car! He loved dancing with me and admired my "beautiful legs!" And too, he did not date other nurses.

So it happened that on December 6, 1941, Barney, his group of friends and I again went to the Pearl Harbor Officers Club for the evening. What an evening it was — full moon, lights, and music, dining and dancing! There were sparkling lights shining from the ships everywhere in the harbor. It was absolutely awesome. A crowded celebration! The great Pacific Fleet was in port for the first time since the 4th of July. The two aircraft carriers were out on assignment. After one of the grandest times I have ever had, Barney drove me to my quarters and we made plans for Waikiki — swimming, movie and dinner at "Trader Vic's" for the following afternoon, Sunday, December 7, 1941. He stood me up!

***

The date was the morning of December 7th and since there were so few patients in the wards, only Irene Boyd and I reported for duty at 7AM. At 7:55, I was making out routine reports and had just given a patient, Sgt. Patton, some aspirin for his headache when we heard a roaring of planes very close by. I remarked, "Sounds like a plane falling." Then, I heard the sound of a great explosion. I screamed, "It crashed!"

Irene, Sgt. Patton and I ran out on the third floor porch that overlooked the barracks, runways, parade grounds, hangars and to our left, Pearl Harbor. Numerous planes were diving—with each setting off an explosion and a great mass of black smoke bellowing from Pearl Harbor. Horrified, I gasped and exclaimed, "My God! It's the Japs!" I couldn't believe it. Someone remarked, "The fleet is in. It must be maneuvers." About that same time the Japs were all over Hickam Field and had laid the first egg in the Hawaiian Air Depot—then we knew! Noise! Deafening noise! More noise!

I rushed downstairs and received permission from the commanding officer, Captain Frank Lane (now Lt. Col.), to bring the patients down. The electricity was off—that meant no elevator. All of the electrical clocks had stopped. The noise was unimaginable with huge blasts from aerial torpedoes, bombs, machine guns and anti-aircraft discharges.

It was bedlam! Within a very short time the bleeding, burned, fractured and dying casualties began pouring in. Many of the injured were coming in on boards, doors and anything that would carry a body. In the middle of all of this, the other nurses and doctors began to arrive.

Everyone was in somewhat of a daze. Chaos! Anger! Fear! Prayers! It was unbelievable! Phrases registered in my mind—phrases I had never heard: "All walking casualties in these trucks to Tripler," then, I wondered what "shrapnel" and "strafing" were. Soon, other military enlisted wives and many other volunteers began arriving to help. We sent them to another wing of the hospital where they began making "wound dressings" by the hundreds.

Up to this time, we were somewhat able to care for the patients by giving them "hypos of morphine" for pain and dressings to cover their torn bleeding wounds. We continued sending them by ambulance, dairy trucks, station wagons and any form of transportation available to Tripler. All the while that incredible noise continued!

Then, we heard the roaring of the planes again. A SECOND ATTACK! We had neither helmets nor gas masks. The bombs were falling closer and closer. BANG! Someone yelled, "DOWN EVERYBODY! DOWN!"

We fell flat on the floor.

The hospital shook—I kept thinking about the cement building crushing in on us and I remember praying. As I fell, I grabbed a large galvanized garbage can lid, which had been lying on the floor, and I quickly slid under it. Someone kept tugging it. I held on! It was Corpsman Mack Montean, who later told me, "Nurse, I wasn't trying to take it from you. I was just trying to get under it with you." The bomb was so close that it made a thirty-foot crater about 40 feet from the right wing of the hospital

The planes passed over and the next bomb fell across the street near the headquarters building. We thought that building was hit until we got up and looked out. And now, smoke and fumes from the bomb came in and someone cried, "Gas!" We all thought the same thing, "…the bombs didn't get us, but the gas will." More casualties arrived which were worse than the first round of wounded and we didn't get a chance to tag them. All we could do was give them a "hypo of morphine," using 10 c.c. syringes, one-quarter grain to each c.c. and sent them off to Tripler.

The porch, where I was working, was literally stacked with casualties. I'll never forget what happened that day. A Major, who was lying on the floor with a bomb fragment in his collarbone signaled with his other arm to stop me when I approached him with a shot of morphine. He said, "Don't stop to take care of me. I'm all right. Give it to the boys who need it."

In another instant, a Corporal called me over to a Sergeant, "Nurse," he exclaimed, "…do something for him quick—he's my 1st Sergeant!" One look and I saw the man in a pool of blood, dead, so I told the Corporal it was too late to try to do anything. Then I covered him with a nearby blanket. The Corporal screamed, "Oh, he can't be! That's my 1st Sergeant! He's too swell a guy—he just can't go." He then broke into convulsive crying and ran out of the hospital and I turned away with a lump in my throat.

There was another wounded soldier, whom I had taken care of while on duty at Tripler a few months prior to this horrific event, who called to me, saying, "Hey, Miss West Florida, can you believe this?" I could hardly recognize him for the dirt and blood on his face. He had to be forced to take a "hypo."

A few moments passed and a Lieutenant called me and asked, "Nurse, if I don't make it, will you tell my wife where the insurance papers are?" So I found an Officer to take the information from him. Later, I learned this Lieutenant lived, but had a leg amputation at Tripler.

There were many casualties who actually walked into the hospital—one with an arm hanging and another with his foot missing. The latter of the two sat holding a cloth tourniquet near his knee and asked, "Nurse, don't I let it bleed about every few minutes?"

In other directions, there were numerous voices crying out, "Water, water," and there was no water. Then, there were the dead who passed through our hospital whose bodies were mangled masses of bone and bloody charred tissue—all too awful to describe. They were placed on the back lawn, checked periodically just in case

Everything around us was burning. We were evacuating the major cases until early afternoon. Water was brought to us in large G.I. cans and the mess hall started functioning—in fact, Hickam was the only active mess hall functioning that day, and we fed hundreds. In the meantime, Red Cross Nurses from Honolulu came out to help, as did quite a few of the military wives and other volunteers. They stayed with us for several days. That night some of them slept in our mess hall.

There are parts of that day for which I can hardly give account. Sometime that afternoon, the nurses and I were driven to our quarters to get clean uniforms. By this time the hospital ward was opened and we were able to work there. But still, the situation could not seem to sink in—the Japs had been here! Our instincts warned us they would probably be back as soon as they refueled and reloaded. After all, this was war—"the real McCoy!" Even while looking at the burning hangars, barracks, bomb craters, and the wreck and ruin of everything on the line, it was hard for me to realize, "I've actually been in a battle, a war, a bombing and I've lived through it!" Thank you, God!

At sunset, "Old Glory" was still flying even though she suffered a huge rip completely across her stripes from an enemy machine gun earlier that morning. There were also bomb craters a few feet from the flag's mast where a machine gun emplacement was now installed. It was unreal!

That night, our first "blackout night" began. Blankets were tacked up on the windows, which were later painted black, and we each had a flashlight covered with blue cellophane. By this time, we were issued helmets and gas masks—WWI vintage! It was eerie, sitting there waiting, listening, and watching. We sat there wondering when another attack would occur.

At about 8:00PM, we heard the sound of planes and thinking they were the enemy, one of the officers commanded, "THEY'RE BACK—EVERYBODY DOWNSTAIRS! GO!" Well, you bet the officer didn't have to say that a second time! We all made a mad rush down the stairs, in the dark, with no electricity. I'm sure I was ahead of everyone who was rushing for fear of falling bombs! I remember being so frightened I couldn't swallow. My mouth was so dry. It was as if in a dream, trying to run for your life, but your feet feel so heavy, they just won't move. That's what it felt like to me.

While rushing down the three flights of steps and reaching what I thought was the ground floor, I started running "straight ahead," but there were actually three more steps to go. Unexpectedly, I fell. From that day, I was left with a severely scraped shin—my only "war wound," which turned into a permanent scar.

Now! More planes! Terrible noise! Anti-aircraft! The entire sky and Oahu was lit up like the 4th of July and Times Square on New Years Eve. What happened was tragic all in itself—Navy airplanes from our aircraft carriers were flying in to Pearl Harbor, unidentified, and sad to say, a few were shot down. For the remainder of that night, we were told to stay on the first floor and rest on the blankets and pillows from the wards. Then later, somewhere into the darkness of that night, a machine gun fired off. This started a rumor that enemy parachute troops had landed and the ground defense was "trigger conscious."

By Tuesday, I had rested enough to begin to think of other things besides patients, the Japanese and myself. I tried to get in touch with Lt. Benning's "outfit" and learned he had moved to another battery just a few miles from Hickam Field. On Wednesday, Barney stopped by the hospital long enough to let me know he was safe, and to say an embracing "hello." He also told me that our friend, Lt. Bill Sylvester was missing and hadn't been accounted for since December 6th, when I spoke with him on the telephone at the Pearl Harbor Officers Club. A few days later, Barney identified a wristwatch and a shredded shirt as Bills. Evidently, while driving through Hickam to get to his station at Fort Kam, Bill was hit by an enemy bomb. Later, a building at Ft. Bliss, El Paso, Texas and a "Minesweeper" were named after Bill as the first Anti-Aircraft Officer killed in action in WWII.

For days, minor cases from shrapnel came in and activities began to once again function normally. We slept in the hospital the first few nights, initially in the officers hospital rooms, then in the X-ray dark room. Within a week or so, we moved to the large beautiful quarters, but by January we were moved to these large, beautiful quarters located at 106 Boquet, directly behind the hospital. This was a charming place for flag officers that had been General Rudolph's, who had since returned to the mainland.

On Thursday, I was able to get a Radiogram off to my parents and to Barney Benning's family saying, "Safe love," that was all! They were received the following Sunday morning, December 14th.

At one point, Barney called to say he was moving to another battery, Fort Barrette, where a Range Officer was needed. I was happy to find that he would only be about a thirty-minute drive from Hickam.

A few weeks later, I received a special written pass from my Chief Nurse and Commanding Officer to visit with Barney at his new post. I had just arrived at the post's Officers' Quarters, (which was actually a small wooden cottage originally built for sugar cane workers, but now "appropriated" by the Army) when an "Air Raid" alarm sounded. Everyone present ran to his battle station and there I stood, ALONE, in this little wooden cottage, now being used as a battery office. The radio announcer kept repeating, "This is a real Air Raid Alarm, take cover." I wondered, "What cover?" Hurriedly, I started looking around the building—it was small and one bomb fragment would have splintered it and me into a thousand pieces. Upon discovering the bathroom, I decided when the bombs started falling nearby, I would get into the tub and pull the mattress off the ODs cot and put it over me with my rosary in hand. With a plan in mind, I went to the door, donned with helmet and gas mask. Now I am READY! Barney had sent word not to be worried, and that everything would be all right. The battery commander came back to me to get more information, (the radio announcer had been keeping me informed) and said to me, "Monica, you let us know what goes on." As it were, every now and then I would shout "…Alarm Still On." Finally, when the announcer said, "…All clear," I excitedly ran to the door and yelled, "…ALL CLEAR!" I further announced, "…false alarm, come out!" Then out came soldiers and officers from everywhere, from what appeared to be bushes and brush but were actually camouflaged guns. I tell this as the tale of the day I COMMANDED a certain post on Oahu, during an Air Raid alarm.

**

On December 17th, I received the following commendation:

```
Subject:  Commendation
To: 2nd Lt. Monica E. Conter, Army Nurse Corps, Station Hospital,
   Hickam Field, T.H.
   Commanding Officer of Station Hospital wishes to congratulate
   and commend the Officers, Nurses, and Enlisted Personnel of
   the Medical Detachment, Hickam Field, upon the brave and
   excellent manner in which each and every one of you performed
   your duties in caring for and evacuating the wounded of this
   Station on the morning of Sunday, 7 December, 1941, while we
   were under the attack of enemy airplanes.

                        Frank H. Lane
                        Captain, Medical Corps.
                        Commanding
```

There were so many things that kept us "war conscious" — the liquor ban, a ten-gallon a month gasoline ration, daylight savings time, nightly blackout, barbed wire and camouflage everywhere. There were "special alerts" when no one was allowed to leave his/her post for days at a time and many "Air Raid" alerts that luckily proved to be false alarms. Instead of wearing hibiscus and leis, we were wearing little tin hats and gas masks. In the mean time, each nurse had arranged with a different medical officer to kill her if the Japanese were to have successful landing and capture Hickam Field, recalling the "Rape of Burma." I chose Captain Raymond L. White.

As the war went on, it seemed my Army Nurse Corps publicity career had not ended. My picture, along with other nurses and personnel assigned there, appeared in the Hickam Highlights, the yearbook Hickam Bomber, and the service paper, The Mid Pacifican. I was titled, "Painkiller."

During these first months after the "Blitz," I saw Barney at least once or twice a week. In late January 1942, he was promoted to First Lieutenant, initiating a big celebration. A trip to Hilo on the "Big Island" — Hawaii, in an Army transport plane, piloted by Capt. Cunningham, was planned. This turned into one of the nicest things that happened to both of us that day in March. I had specially arranged the trip so Barney could be included.

That same month, two medical doctors, Lt. Cmdr. Samuel Guillard and Lt. Cmdr. Tom R. Meeker — the very ones who taught me while at nursing school in Providence Hospital, Mobile, Alabama, reported for duty at the Pearl Harbor Naval Hospital. It was really great being with them again. (Note: Dr. Gillard would later become part of our marriage ceremony.)

Soon thereafter, a milestone was set. It was now April 2, 1942, where "the largest mass decoration in the history of the U.S. Army" occurred at Hickam Field. The nurses, now eight, who were stationed at Hickam Hospital, participated. With the use of wheelchairs, each nurse rolled the still disabled patients out onto and down the runway, near the Hickam Control Towers, to receive their awards. Each patient received both Silver Stars and Purple Hearts. The nurses received beautiful red carnation leis. Technicolor films recorded this occasion under the able direction of Lt. Commander John Ford (director of "How Green Was My Valley"). As far as I know these films were never released to the public. After the ceremony, the nurses accepted an invitation to a delightful luncheon at the home of Brigadier General Willis Hale, who later became Major General, AUS (Army of the United States).

When Easter arrived, I received a lovely orchid lei from Barney. A few days later he was transferred to the Hickam Field gate area (this is where an anti-aircraft gun from the damaged battleship California was emplaced). By this time, I had decided I wouldn't date anyone else and so we were together every night. One day, he asked me if I loved the Army so much that I would never be willing to give up my career. I responded with, "Why?" and he replied with, "Well, you never know—someday someone might ask you to marry." (Now, hear this!)

It was just about the same time that I learned the letter I had written to Colonel Flikke (Superintendent of the Army Nurse Corps), regarding December 7, that "infamous day," had been published in several nursing journals. The same letter was read over the radio and at many Army medical meetings and conventions as well.

In June, Barney was transferred to another nearby military post. This was about the same time the "Battle of Midway," our big victorious battle, occurred! It seemed everyone we knew sank an enemy battleship or carrier, even though our losses were very heavy. As a result of this victory, the Islands celebrated! Officers were given a three-day pass every 60 days so Barney and I planned ours for the early part of July. With anticipation, I thought "…Oh, he is waiting for his birthday, July 6th and then he will propose."

As it turned out, two very good friends of ours, Larry and Celene Twomey, invited us to be their overnight guests. They were a young married couple with an apartment at 1116 Wilder Avenue, in Honolulu. Our passes were for July 6th through the 8th. On July 6th, they had a lovely birthday dinner for Barney—complete with cake, candles, gifts and more. However, for me, with no proposal, I was disappointed. Nonetheless, it was a happy birthday for my sweetheart Barney.

The next day, most of our time was spent swimming at Waikiki with our host and hostess and another couple, Lt. Alex Mitchell and Margarete Benevites. That evening, while the two of us were sitting on the lanai, Barney was getting rather sentimental. He asked if I loved him, and if so, why? After stuttering for a period of time, I finally managed to put into words several reasons I loved him. (There really were so many—it was quite hard to tell them all.) Then, when I asked him the same question, he told me—without hesitating, exactly 12 reasons. (I always thought he must have rehearsed this.) When the evening ended, I was once again disappointed.

Purple Heart ceremony at Hickam Field

Decoration of Patients

*Old Glory Still Flying
– Dec.7, 1941*

*Hickam Highlights,
Monica "Painkiller"
Jan. 1942*

Twomey Sofa–
Barney
proposes marriage
July 7, 1942

Nurses Quarters

Waikiki Beach
7/6/1942

The next morning when I was going through the living room I saw Barney sitting there. He must have awakened early, or at least I hoped he had. He called me and we started making plans for the day. Finally, he said, "That was some snow job you gave me last night—all those reasons." I replied, "Well, you didn't do so badly yourself!" I felt myself getting a little uncomfortable. "Monica," he said, as he paused, looking intensely at me, and continued, "I want one of those mints on the table." I said, "Yes, lover," even though I knew he didn't like mints. Then he said, "Monica, put your head on my shoulder." I did, with my heart nearly pounding out of my chest. This was really it, I knew it—I just knew it! Finally, he said, "Monica, do you love me enough to be my wife?" I was almost crying from happiness. All I could do was shake my head in the affirmative. Then he said, "Well, Monica?" I swallowed hard, and then hesitated (I couldn't catch my breath for the life of me and I was nearly choking). "Will you marry me?" I threw my arms around him and said in a voice I hardly recognized as my own, "Oh Barney, I thought you would never ask!" He impatiently demanded, "Well, will you? You haven't said you will!" I replied, "Oh darling, yes, you know I will." Then after a loving and lengthy discussion, we set the date for August 20th, 1942.

During the following six weeks, I was simply walking on air. There was so much to be done—permission to be obtained from the Military Governor, an apartment to be found in Honolulu (very scarce), a trousseau to be bought, letters to our families, engagement announcements in several newspapers back home, and the like. It seemed a million things had to be done. I had to arrange for the chapel wedding and plan for the wedding reception breakfast with all of its details. There were no parents nearby to assist—only my nurse friends. I did, however, have great help from my bridesmaid, M. Kathleen Coberly, who was absolutely wonderful.

The wedding day finally arrived and for as much of it as I can remember, it seemed very special and lovely. The following clipping from the Honolulu Advertiser has helped to refresh my memory:

"At a nuptial Mass at the Post Chapel of Hickam Field last Thursday, August 20, 1942, Miss Monica E. Conter, daughter of Dr. and Mrs. August E. Conter of Apalachicola, Florida, was married to Lt. Bernard F. Benning, U.S. Army, son of Mr. and Mrs. Harry J. Benning of Niles, Michigan. Chaplain Maurice A. Mullan, U.S. Army, performed the ceremony in a setting of palms, calla and Easter Lilies and lighted tapers in gold candelabra. The traditional wedding selections were played and Miss Marie Galloway, Capt. J.F. Schooling, U.S. Army and Capt. Charles Dugan, S.S. Army sang nuptial hymns.

The bride, who was escorted to the altar by Lt. Commander Samuel Gaillard, MCUSNR, was gowned in white slipper satin fashioned with sweetheart neck and long sleeves tapering at the wrists, and designed in long torso style with a full skirt falling into a court train. Her fingertip veil of misty tulle was secured to a satin Juliet cap accented by orange blossoms. As her only jewelry, she wore a pearl necklace, gift of the bridegroom. She carried a bouquet of white orchids and gardenias to which were fastened pikake leis.

Miss Mary Kathleen Coberly was maid of honor and only attendant. She was frocked in a gold colored taffeta and chiffon gown styled with long, full sleeves and swirling skirt. She wore a matching toque and her flowers were lavender orchids.

For her going away costume, the bride selected a yellow sports ensemble detailed with green accessories and an orchid corsage.

Capt. Lawrence Twomey, U.S. Army, was the best man.

After the ceremony, a wedding breakfast was held at the Hickam Field Nurses Quarters, arranged with palms, white lilies and ginger. The bride cut her tiered wedding cake with her husband's saber in accordance with the traditional military custom.

The young couple will be at home at 1116 Wilder Avenue after a honeymoon at Waikiki's Halekalani Hotel.

The bride was graduated from Convent of Mercy, St. Patrick's High School in Apalachicola and Providence Hospital in Mobile, Alabama. She also attended Spring Hill College. She has been stationed at Hickam Field with the Army Nurse Corps for the past year. Prior to her tour of duty on Oahu, she was at the Walter Reed General Hospital in Washington, D.C.

The bridegroom was graduated from Michigan State College and is a member of Tau Beta Pi and Phi Kappa Tau. He is stationed at Fort Kamehameha, T.H."

Wedding held in "Temporary Chapel"
Aug. 20, 1942,
(Chapel was destroyed Dec. 7th).
Cake cut with Barney's sword,
Wedding guests,
and our Wedding Party
(Entrikin, Boyd, Pomerance, Benevites,
Col. Arens, and Twomey)

"The Palace"
Nurses' Quarters (for 6!), 601 Boquet

Honeymoon Bride–
Aug 21, 1942 at
1116 Wilder Avenue

Among the many lovely presents I received, some of the most useful gifts were several gasoline ration cards. That was something that money couldn't buy. On our honeymoon, we enjoyed many beautiful drives that we were now able to take due to our friend's thoughtfulness.

Up to the present time (when this was first written), all Army nurses who married would automatically be separated from the Service with an honorable discharge. As it turned out, while on my 38 days of final accrued leave (living in Honolulu as a civilian), an order came from the Surgeon General, U.S. Army, "recalling to duty all Army nurses who were on terminal leave by reason of marriage." On September 23rd, I reported back to Station Hospital, Hickam Field as one of the first married nurses on active duty in the Army Nurse Corps.

At first, I cannot say I was any too happy about the situation. The thought of moving all my "belongings" back to Hickam was a headache in itself. I soon realized, however, that I would be able to see Barney everyday, as his duty station was less than a five-minute drive away from my quarters at Hickam.

One day, we received a message saying, "Sometime in the early part of next summer, you will receive a little bundle—I hope it's a boy." Signed: The Stork. (The rabbit test was positive.) Was Barney ever "cocky," being recently promoted to Captain and learning of his expectant fatherhood, all at the same time! I thought he would never stop celebrating and bragging.

In a few days, because of my physical condition, I wrote my official request for "Separation from Military Service." I then started "sweatin' it out," as it is commonly called in military language. I thought my orders for discharge and evacuation back to the Mainland would never arrive. I just knew I would be on a ship convoy for Christmas and too, I kept thinking, "…the Jap bombs didn't get me, but their submarine torpedoes will!" If I couldn't be with Barney, then I wanted to be with my parents in Florida. On Tuesday, December 15th, I gave up hoping and started corresponding with my parents that there was no way for me to be home for the holidays.

That same evening, one of our nurses was called on "special duty" with a Colonel Hans C. Adamson—his identity was a military secret! The following morning, I was assigned to that "special duty." We eventually learned the "special duty" was with one of Captain Eddie Rickenbacker's rescued crewmembers that had just arrived from "down under" following their 21 days on a raft. Sgt. James Reynolds was the other rescued patient. That night I couldn't sleep—the last time I looked at the clock it was 2:20AM. I kept wishfully dreaming how wonderful it would be if I could fly home—to be there for Christmas and avoid that long dangerous convoy trip. Above all, I was also longing for the opportunity to ride with "Captain Eddie," such an international hero, a WWI Ace—an honor in itself.

The next morning, after being on duty a few hours, I felt a spontaneous desire to speak with the Naval doctor, Lt. Cmdr. John Durkin, who was not only caring for my patient, the Colonel, but who was also preparing this patient for travel back to the mainland—Walter Reed General Hospital, Washington D.C., for further medical treatment. I just had to know if there was the slightest possibility that I might fly to the States with them, "…couldn't you use a nurse?" I asked. Both he and my patient laughed—they thought I was joking, so I let the matter drop. They were leaving in the afternoon at five o'clock.

As the morning went on, Capt. Eddie visited us. While there, he asked me about my experiences on December 7th. While conversing, we also spoke about a mutual friend, "Dr. Ralph Nelson Green, Chief Physician for Eastern Airlines, of which Capt. Eddie was President. Dr. Green and my father, Dr. A.E. Conter were Associates at one time. I remember visiting the Greens as a teenager at Challen Avenue (Riverside), when they resided in Jacksonville, Florida.

After reporting off duty at 2:00 PM, I went to my quarters to take a rest. At 3:45 PM Barney called and said to get dressed as, "…we are going to Fort Shafter Club for dinner and guess what else? Your departure orders have arrived." At 4:00 PM, the nurse on duty telephoned and said, "Monica, come to the hospital right away—something is stewing." So over I went. I was to see Dr. Durkin, the Naval doctor—the same one I spoke with earlier. I told him of my good fortune in that, my orders to be released from the service had just been published and I was to return to the mainland on the first available transportation. This was understood to mean the first convoy out—only "active-duty service men" were allowed to fly, which meant I had to leave on "other" transportation from Hawaii to the Mainland. I spoke to the doctor and made him understand I was really serious and that all I was waiting for was transportation. He went to the phone and spoke to Capt. Rickenbacker, who in turn stated he would have to make some calls about getting permission for me. Well, in a few minutes—that seemed like hours, he called back and said I COULD GO! Once again, as seen numerous times throughout my 3-year military career, I felt my Good Angel was up there rootin' for me. You should have seen me hug that doctor! I was crying, laughing and jumping up and down all at the same time. It was then that I realized I had no time for that—I had only one hour to get ready and get over to the plane.

In the meantime, I called Barney and told him of the "happenings." I had barely arrived at my quarters when he arrived. Everyone was there helping me get ready and packed. I was too excited for words! I recall hearing one nurse say, "You won't believe it—I know of three times I have seen Monica put that handkerchief in her suitcase." When I had calmed down enough to tell Barney the details, I said, "You see, this is what I mean when I say things just happen to me this way." He said in his Yankee manner, "Well, you know Lover, (he also called me Queen Mother and/or Iron Magnolia, depending on the circumstance) nothing did happen for so many years down there in Apalachicola, Florida. It's just catching up with you." I would have "told him off," but I realized what he said was quite true.

Well, as it was, the time for departure was extended to 8:00 PM, giving me a little more time to get dressed and packed. Now, while at the Hickam Officer's Club with Barney, I couldn't eat for the life of me! I was too full of every kind of emotion—thoughts that these were the last few minutes I would spend with Barney for weeks, months, maybe even years! Why, maybe—never. This would also be the last few moments I would spend on the Island I loved—I was leaving behind people, places and events that would be in my memory forever. Yet, apparently, I was in a daze. I just couldn't talk to Barney. I couldn't tell him all of the million thoughts that were rushing through my mind.

Just before we left the car to walk over to the plane, he asked, "Do you think Hawaii is a very romantic place?" I replied, "Romantic? Well a husband and that isn't all—yes, quite romantic!" At that moment, my heart began to break, very seriously as he kissed me goodbye and he said, "Darling, regardless of what ever happens, never forget you are my wife." You can be sure several minutes elapsed before I was able to leave for the plane.

Next, the excitement of flower leis and last minute farewells seized the moment. As I stood in the door of the plane and stopped to look back, there was Barney. I threw him a kiss then rushed in to find my seat in the new B-24. Looking out of the window beside me—the engines had started and people were standing off near the hangar, I scanned the crowd to catch a last glimpse of that Captain of mine and there he was, waving. Blinding tears streamed down my face as the plane pulled away and I waved my final, "Aloha."

The trip to the mainland was uneventful. During the night, I would awaken and look out the window to see nothing but water, sky, stars and the moon. I would also anxiously glance at the two engines outside my window and wonder and pray if they were okay. My two patients were doing nicely—except for the occasional sip of water and pain medication; there was nothing to be done for them.

Loading 2 patients, Col. Hans Adamson and Sgt. James Reynolds
for transportation to the mainland.

Captain Eddie Rickenbacker with crew and Lt. Monica Conter
Benning ANC, Hamilton Field, CA – Dec. 17, 1942

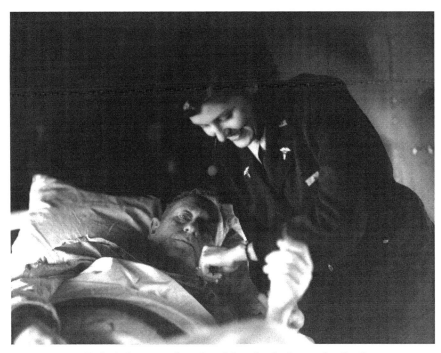

Col. Adamson having his vital signs checked

We arrived at Hamilton Field, California in time for lunch the following day. About 3:30 PM, I went into the city of San Francisco for dinner at the St. Francis Hotel as a guest of the Naval doctor, Dr. Durkin. There we ran into Capt. Cherry, who was piloting Capt. Rickenbacker's plane when they and the other crewmembers crashed in the Pacific. What a small world! While riding back across the Golden Gate Bridge I thought about how much had happened in my life since I last saw it over seventeen months ago. Tragic! Beautiful! Unforgettable! Happy! Thankful!

Around noon the following day, we left for Washington, D.C., stopping at Burbank, California to refuel and to see Captain Rickenbacker's mother and brother, Rosalind Russell and her husband, Major Brysson, who were both close friends of my patient, the Colonel. She was very gracious and remarked to me that she felt, "Army Nurses are the unsung heroes of this war."

We then continued on with our cross-country trip, making just one stop to refuel at Love Field, Dallas, Texas. That Saturday morning, when we landed at Bolling Field, Washington D.C., there were ambulances to meet the plane. The ambulance took Colonel Adamson to Walter Reed General Hospital. It is impossible to describe how forever grateful I was to Captain Rickenbacker for such a wonderful trip.

I signed in at Delano Hall, the beautiful ANC Quarters where I spent my first one and a half years stationed at Walter Reed General Hospital. It was at this very place that I had my entrance physical exam, my first day of duty with the ANC, and now — to have my FINAL "honorable discharge," effective December 29, 1942, brought it all to fruition. Looking around, there were only a few familiar faces among the nurses that I recognized. Wartime causes many changes, especially after seventeen months.

While in Washington, one thing I wanted to see was a "good snow." It would be nice to see a real heavy snowfall just once before going south. I went to sleep thinking this in the back of my mind, then woke up Sunday morning with everything covered in snow, four-inches thick! It was quite a contrast to the "summer" in Hawaii I had just left only a few days before. Once again, it made me thankful for the number of good fortunes I've experienced and the protective "One" above, the Good Angel.

On Monday morning, I went to Walter Reed for my "discharge physical." Later, I was invited to have lunch with Colonel Flikke. While waiting to see her, I recalled that just about three years ago, I stood in her office asking about the possibilities of my joining the Army Nurse Corps. Little did I know then of all it held in store for me — and now, here I was waiting to tell her goodbye and to leave the great organization that she still represents. While we were at lunch, she asked me to write the story of my Army Career. She wanted me to include my modeling (with her) from 1940 through mid-1941, while recruiting Red Cross Nurses to join the Army Nurse Corps. She wanted an account of my experiences during the Japanese attack on December 7, 1941 along with my romance and marriage to Barney, and my trip to the mainland with Capt. Eddie Rickenbacker. Now, you have it!

That afternoon when I called National Airport for plane reservations to Tallahassee, Florida on Eastern Airlines, I learned that I could depart on the same night. You see, Capt. Rickenbacker had arranged for my "priority" on one of his planes, au gratis. I had thanked him profusely for his thoughtfulness and his kindness to me once again.

It was with an emotional prayer when I ran into my Daddy's arms the next morning in Tallahassee. There were many times I wondered if I would ever see him, my mother, brother and sister again. I said, "Daddy, you surely must have been praying for me." He replied, "Honey, you bet — every night."

As we drove to Apalachicola, I could hardly recognize the highway I had once known by heart. There were Army camps everywhere. Even at home, the streets were simply "buzzing" with Service people in uniform. It was great being with the family and seeing old friends once again. It made me think, less than a week before, I had left Hawaii, spent one day in San Francisco and three days in Washington, D.C. — it was just all too fantastic! Unbelievable! Thanks to the Good Angel!

My brother, Charles, at the time was stationed in Miami with the military police, and my sister, Alice Maria (also known as "Doll") was here at home, having just finished high school. I had barely entered our home when my parents showed me a book titled, None More Courageous, by Stewart Holbrook. It was a book about American War Heroes of Today. In his chapter, "Young Women at War," there were several pages concerning my part in the "Blitz" on December 7th, 1941. It said in part: "…her father, Augustus E. Conter, M.D. back in small Apalachicola, Florida, could have reason to be proud of her." McMillan Company published the book in November of 1942, one month before I was honorably discharged and returned home.

Down to the telegraph office I rushed. I had to get a Radiogram off to my lover, Barney, as I had promised. The following message was sent:

```
          Arrived safely Merry Christmas

                    Love.

          Monica Conter Benning
```

***

On June 5, 2006, Bernard F. Benning Lt. Col., USAR was buried at Arlington National Cemetery, Washington D.C. with full military honors.

None More Courageous

AMERICAN WAR HEROES OF TODAY

by

STEWART H. HOLBROOK

New York

THE MACMILLAN COMPANY · 1942

Title Page in None More Courageous (1942)
S.H. Holbrook included references to Monica Conter & Family

Contents of Appendix

HONORING MONICA AND BERNARD BENNING

- [Begin Insert]

Mr. BURNS. Mr. President, today I rise in honor of Monica Conter Benning and Bernard Floyd Benning, Barney, on the celebration of their 61st wedding anniversary on August 20, 2003. Monica and Barney are the only surviving couple of the Pearl Harbor attack who both were in the immediate Pearl Harbor area at the time of the bombing. As the courtship between these two officers evolved in the setting of World War II, their experiences during the attack on America, December 7, 1941, are an important part of American history.

Barney, a college ROTC 2nd Lt. from Niles, MI, was ordered to active duty to Hawaii in May 1941. Barney joined an anti-aircraft battery in Fort Kamehameha at the entrance of the Pearl Harbor channel.

Army nurse 2nd Lt. Monica Conter of Apalachicola, FL served at Walter Reed General Hospital in 1940-1941, and was the official model for the Army Nurse Corps Recruiting Program. Monica was later assigned to the new Hickam Field Hospital, adjacent to Pearl Harbor and separate by a lone chain link fence. Monica is the only nurse still living today who was on duty at Hickam Field Hospital at the time of the attack. During the attack on December 7th, a bomb fell on the hospital lawn about 60 feet from the building, leaving a large crater. A banyon tree sapling was planted in the crater several days after the attack. Today, beside the huge tree is a granite monument and plaque, honoring Monica's service as an Army nurse on duty that fateful day.

Monica and Barney Benning first met on a prearranged ``blind date'' in September 1941; the beginning of a lifetime together. Their courtship continued with regularity until that ``Day of Infamy,'' December 7, 1941--the first terrorist attack on America. The following Wednesday, when Barney appeared at Hickam Hospital in a dirty, wrinkled uniform, it was quite an emotional moment when they found each other alive.

``Off Duty'' time was infrequent and often they were miles apart and usually on some kind of alert status until the American victory at the Battle of Midway in May.

They wed on August 20, 1942, in the temporarily camouflaged Hickam Field Chapel; the original chapel was destroyed on December 7.

On August 20, 2003, they will celebrate their 61st wedding anniversary. I congratulate and praise this couple, members of our Greatest Generation, for serving America to protect our precious democracy. I applaud your bravery and dedication to preserving freedom for all Americans.

Monica and Barney currently reside in Fort Myers, FL. They have two sons, Phil Benning and Gregory Benning and a daughter, Veronica Benning, as well as two grandchildren, Melanie and Lauren Benning.

Congressional Record & Additional Statements

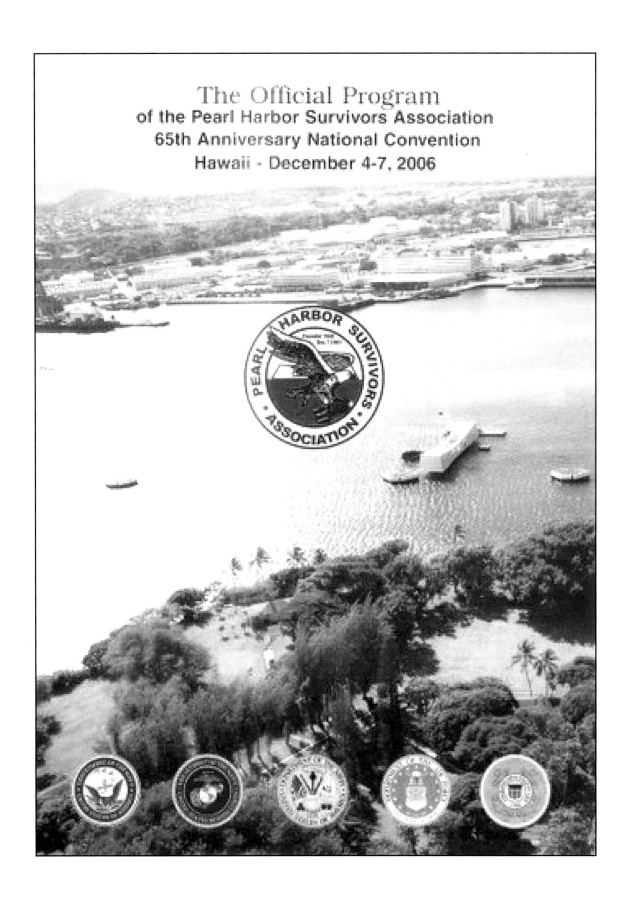

The Official Program
of the Pearl Harbor Survivors Association
65th Anniversary National Convention
Hawaii - December 4-7, 2006

December 15, 2006

Dear Lieutenant Benning:

On behalf of the entire Army Nurse Corps, I wish to take this opportunity to thank you for your dedicated service during World War II. Today's Army Nurse Corps stands firmly on the foundation laid by the lineage of Army Nurses like you who selflessly served our Nation since the conception of our Corps in 1901.

You are most deserving of the honor bestowed upon you on December 7th, for your lifesaving care to Service members wounded by the attack on Pearl Harbor.

We are forever grateful. Please accept the Chief of the Army Nurse Corps' *Coin of Excellence* as a token of our appreciation.

Very Respectfully,

Gale S. Pollock
Major General, AN
Chief, Army Nurse Corps

Lieutenant Monica Benning
U.S. Army Retired
2674 Winkler Avenue
Ft. Myers, Florida 33901

Letter from Army Nurse Corps

December 7, 2006

Dear Mrs. Benning

On behalf of the men and women of the Total Nursing Force and Air Force Medical Service, I would like to extend a heartfelt and sincere thank you for your service to the Army Nurse Corps from 1940 to 1943. Though you were on active duty just a few short years, you helped lead the way for the future of both the Army Nurse Corps and the Air Force Nurse Corps.

Your service on 7 December 1941 was an extraordinary example for all nurses to follow. As a 2d Lt, you triaged and cared for the wounded while bombs were exploding nearby. You quickly learned how to fashion bandages from sheets and clothing, and how to comfort the wounded and dying through words and your touch. Your bravery in times of crisis will never be forgotten. Due to your superior care for your patients, you were specifically asked to tend to Capt Eddie Rickenbacker and his injured crewmembers as they were flown back to the mainland. Your story of that infamous day in December of 1941 will be an inspiration to all military nurses being deployed in our present, and any future wars. You are truly a model for military-nurse recruitment.

While words can never fully define your contributions to the Army and Air Force Nurse Corps, and the patients you served during WWII, you clearly played a vital role in shaping the future of the greatest military Nurse Corps in the world. Once again, thank you for all you have done for us and the nurses following in your footsteps.

Sincerely

MELISSA A. RANK
Major General, USAF, NC, SFN
Assistant Surgeon General, Nursing Services
Office of the Surgeon General

Letter from Air Force Nurse Corps

December 07, 2006

Hawai'i
Navy News

Serving the "Best Homeport in the Navy"

Brokaw meets nurse from 'Greatest Generation'

U.S. Navy photo by MCC Don Bra

Former NBC Nightly News anchorman Tom Brokaw grabs a photo opportunity with (Army) 2nd Lt. Monica C. Benning who is the last living nurse that was at Hickam Field on Dec. 7. Over 3,000 survivors and guests were at the annual observance of the Dec. 7, 1941 attack on Pearl Harbor as U.S. Navy/National Park Service conducted a joint ceremony commemorating the 65th anniversary of the attack on Pearl Harbor. The theme of this year's historic commemoration 'A Nation Remembers' reflected on how the remembrance of Pearl Harbor has evolved throughout the years since World War II.

Tom Brokaw & Monica Conter Benning
"Brokaw meets nurse from 'Greatest Generation'"

23 August 2000

Monica Conter Benning
1498 Goldrush Ave
Melbourne, FL 32940

Dear Monica,

I am Lt Col Ruth M. Anderson, The Chief nurse at the 15th Medical Group (formerly Hickam Station Hospital), Hickam Air Force Base, Hawaii. Sara Entrikin gave me your address. I called her because I am very interested in learning more about nurses who worked at Hickam Station Hospital during World War II. I am extremely happy to have obtained your address.

In 1997 our clinic was dedicated in memory of Lt (Dr.) William Schick. He was a flight surgeon that had been a passenger on one of the B-17s that landed on Oahu on 7 Dec 41 unaware that the island was being bombed. He died of shrapnel wounds later that day after being transferred to Tripler. In addition, just a few weeks ago, we dedicated a conference room in the clinic in memory of Lt Annie Fox, the head nurse of Hickam Hospital in Dec 41. It is named in her honor... but will contain all the history I can find on all doctors/nurses/medics that were assigned to the hospital during World War II. It will also contain the history of military nurses serving on Oahu during WW II. I visit the History Office here frequently trying to dig up more information about the medical facility. I even went to several meetings of the Department of Hawaii, Order of the Purple Heart to see if I could get some help from them. However, it sure has been difficult trying to locate nurses who were actually here at the time.

I have met the sons of both Lt Schick and Dr. Garrett (not sure what his rank was); and I also have a script that was written by Capt Frank Lane, the Hickam Hospital commander at the time. But, I would cherish any first-hand accounts I can get from those that served here during those early days of the war. I would really like to get copies of anything you have that tells your story or the story of other military nurses.

Also, Lt Gen Trapp, our current pacific Air Forces Vice Commander, Lives in a house across the street from the clinic (the hospital I think you assigned to). He learned that nurses may have lived in his house during World War II and wants to validate this information and learn more about the nurses who live there. After talking to Sara, I think it is the same house, but I don't know for sure, possible you can help me. If you lived in the house with the other nurses, possibly you could describe it for me... it is on Boquet Blvd. Eventually, I should be able to send you pictures of how it looked in 1941 and how it looks today to help us identify the right home.

I am really looking forward to receiving anything you can send (historical accounts, pictures, etc.)... I will definitely make copies of everything and return them to you immediately (unless you tell me that what you send are copies for me to keep). I will reimburse you for any/all expenses.

Thank you (mahalo) ahead of time for any information you can send, I am absolutely thrilled that I found you!

RUTH M. ANDERSON, Lt Col, USAF, NC
Commander, 15th Medical operations Squadron
Chief Nurse, 15th Medical Group

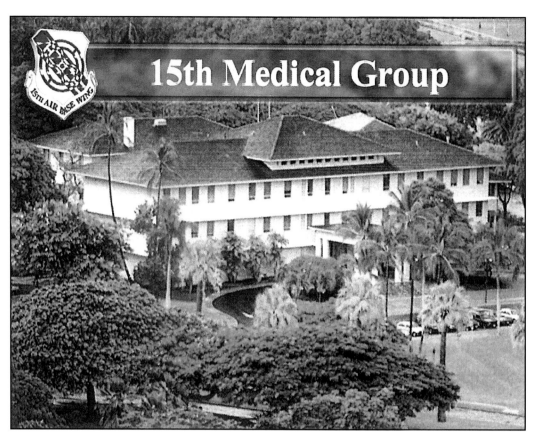

Welcome
Lt Monica Conter Benning
A Great American Hero
to
the 15th Medical Group
Hickam Air Force Base, Hawaii

8 December 2006

MEMORANDUM FOR 15 MDG/CC

2 6 APR 2001

FROM: 15 ABW/CC

SUBJECT: Dedication of the Banyan Tree to Mrs. (2Lt) Monica Conter Benning

1. The 15th Medical Group is authorized to dedicate the banyan tree adjacent to the clinic, between the Commander's parking lot and Boquet Avenue to Mrs. (2Lt) Monica Conter Benning. This authorization is permissible IAW AFI 36-3108, Section A.1., "Memorialization Program and Ceremonies."

2. Mrs. Monica Conter Benning (2Lt Monica Conter while assigned to Hickam Field) was one of six registered nurses who had been transferred from other Oahu Army hospitals to the brand new Hickam Station Hospital on 15 Nov 41. She was one of two nurses (and the only one still alive today) who was on duty when the bombs began falling on December 7th. They were joined by most of the other staff members that morning and worked non-stop to care for hundreds of wounded troops brought to the new 30-bed hospital. One 500 pound bomb fell just yards from the front wing of the building. Two weeks later, a banyan tree was planted in that bomb crater as a healing gesture. Mrs. Conter Benning was present the day this tree was planted and has seen it mature and thrive through the years.

3. Through this dedication, we recognize Mrs. Conter Benning and all men and women who have served their country as well as the bravery of the people of Oahu on December 7th, 1941. This dedication will also serve to protect this tree from future demolition.

JOHN M. WEST, Colonel, USAF
Commander, 15th Air Base Wing

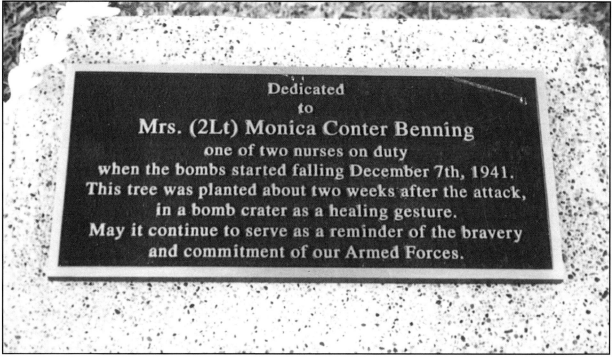

Dedicated
to
Mrs. (2Lt) Monica Conter Benning
one of two nurses on duty
when the bombs started falling December 7th, 1941.
This tree was planted about two weeks after the attack,
in a bomb crater as a healing gesture.
May it continue to serve as a reminder of the bravery
and commitment of our Armed Forces.

Dedication of the Banyan Tree by Dept of the Air Force
(L to R: Major Beth Ewing USAF, Lt. Col. Ruth Anderson USAF, Ret., Ms. Belinda Zimmerer)

50

WALTER LORD
116 EAST 68TH STREET
NEW YORK, N. Y. 10021

September 19, 1991

Mrs. Monica Conter Benning
4483 Windjammer Lane
Ft. Myers, FL 33919

Dear Mrs. Benning,

How thoughtful of you to send me those pictures of
our meeting in Austin! As the very first person mentioned in
Day of Infamy, you and Barney have a special place in my
affections, and it meant a lot to me too to finally meet you.

I also expect to be in Pearl Harbor on December 7,
we must make a point of trying to meet for a little while
anyhow. At present I don't know my schedule or even where I'll
be staying. Meanwhile, do get in touch, if you and Barney are
in New York. My phone number is: 212 628-9192.

All best wishes to you both.

Cordially,

Walter Lord

Walter Lord's Sept 19, 1991 Letter
Insert of Photo, L-R: Monica, Walter Lord & Barney

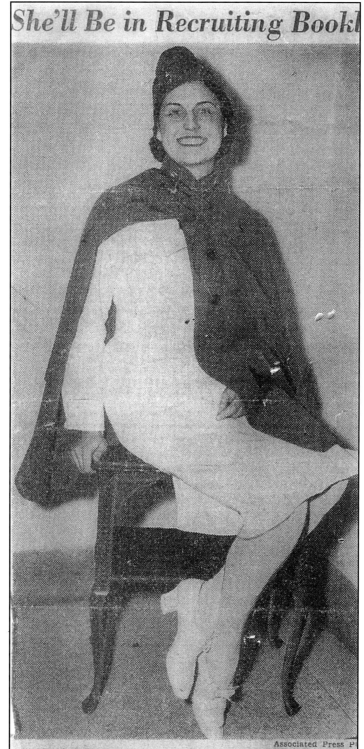

Associated Press P

MODEL NURSE—Miss Monica Conter, on duty at Walt
Reed Hospital, models an Army nurse's uniform for a pi
ture which will appear in a nurse recruiting booklet bei
issued by the American Red Cross

L HARBOR'S
LIFE LOVE
Y

How romance blossomed amid the bomb blasts

damaged and 188 airplanes were destroyed on the ground.

The Japanese lost fewer than 100 men, 29 planes and six submarines.

As Barney bravely toiled at his duties, he had no way of knowing if Monica was alive.

"I could see the hospital was still standing, but that's about all," he says. "There were no phones or electricity and I couldn't leave my post."

Monica was in the same predicament. All she could see was the charred remains of her sweetheart's encampment.

But just like in a movie, they were dramatically united three days later. Still slaving away in the hospital, Monica was stunned when the doors suddenly flew open. "There he was," she says, "the ugliest, filthiest soldier you ever saw. Even the movies could never have made him up like that!"

The couple flew into each other's arms – and they refused to let the war get in the way of their happiness.

Barney proposed on his birthday – July 6 – and the couple used two three-day passes to honeymoon in the Hale Kulani Hotel.

After the war, Barney and Monica continued to live happily ever after.

He became an executive for a power company, while Monica became a model before establishing her as a timeshare saleswoman.

They had three children together, and are now grandparents.

And they thoroughly enjoyed the film that is partially based on their own romance – which Barney has seen.

"While Monica says "Pearl Harbor movie – is just wonderful," Barney says: "The battle scenes are authentic, but not so sure about the romance. Hollywood just got the real

TIMELESS ROMANCE
The cinematic love affair between Kate Beckinsale and Ben Affleck (above) was based on the real-life romance between Monica and Barney Benning

53

REMEMBERING PEARL HARBOR:

Last of
her kind

Former Army Nurse was one of the few
women on duty in Hawaii on Day of Infamy

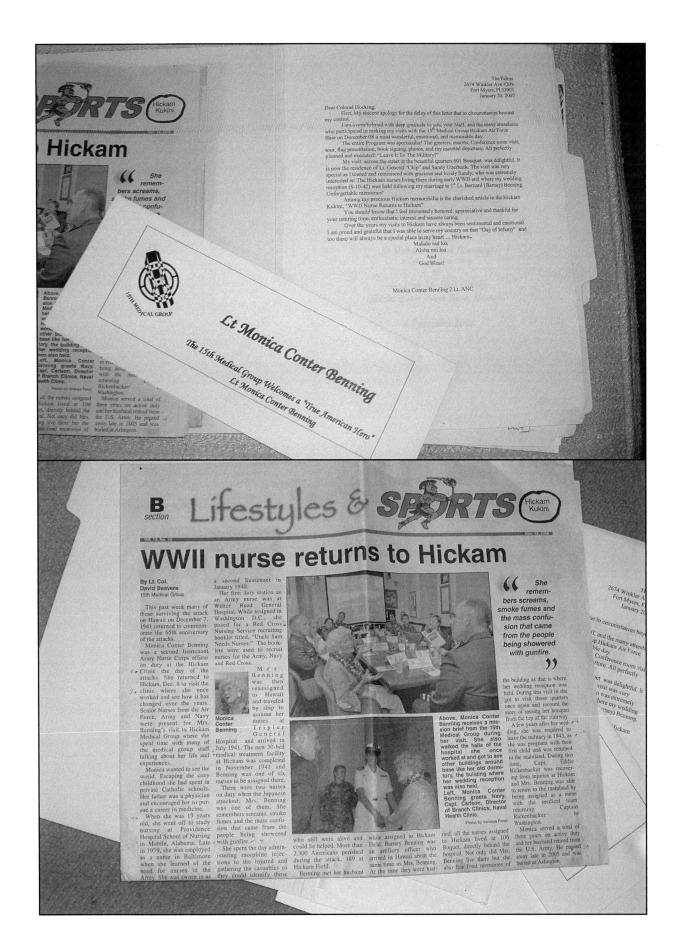

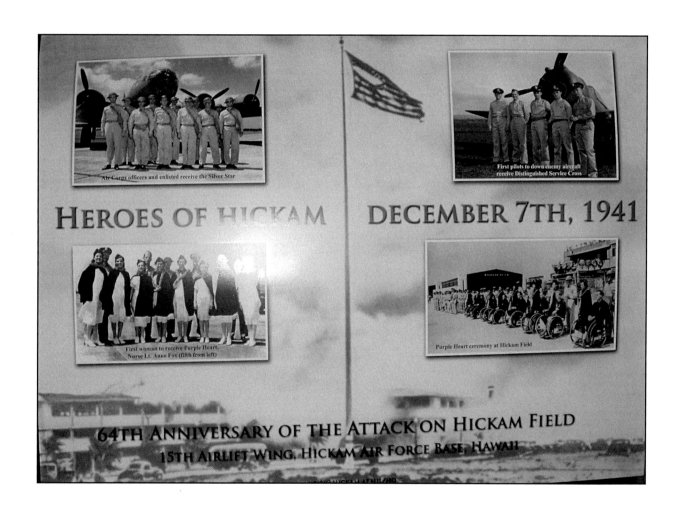

HEROES OF HICKAM DECEMBER 7TH, 1941

Air Corps officers and enlisted receive the Silver Star

First pilots to down enemy aircraft receive Distinguished Service Cross

First woman to receive Purple Heart, Nurse Lt. Anne Fox (fifth from left)

Purple Heart ceremony at Hickam Field

64TH ANNIVERSARY OF THE ATTACK ON HICKAM FIELD
15TH AIRLIFT WING, HICKAM AIR FORCE BASE, HAWAII

CLINT KRAUSE/THE NEWS-PRESS

...ophy around City of Palms Park in Fort

...ers

... current
... sat on
...ld so did
...ers John
... Tammy

... was about

... round of
...kickoff to
... told the
...e dubbed
... Monday
...ermed a

...x fans had
...about how
...in a World
...rk Yanke
...ormenting

news-press.com

■ See a photo gallery from Monday night's festivities and read stories from Sunday's four-page special section on this week's Red Sox celebrations in Southwest Florida.

INSIDE SPORTS

■ Tim Wakefield and Mike Timlin, two members of the World Series champion Red Sox, talk about the historic series win and look ahead to next season **C4**
■ More photos from Monday night's rally **C6**
■ Pitcher Derek Lowe of Fort Myers wasn't at Monday's event **C7**

...ioxx in study

... study. "What
... is that all cox-2
...ay not be the

... funded by the
...oth drugs and
...ernment, was
...al Medicine
... surveyed 1,718
...the five-county
... area who had
...and were treat-
...6 hospitals, and

a comparison group of 6,800 people in the region.
The chances of having a heart attack were 272 times greater in Vioxx users, the researchers said. than in Celebrex.
But the researchers also found that patients using either drug were not at a significantly greater risk of having a heart attack than those who did not use either drug.

Holiday Sale!
Hundreds of rolls, room size, remnants and area rugs in stock.
3120 Metro Parkway • Ft. Myers, FL
(239) 332.5498 • email flooltalk.net

UP TO 60% OFF
Instock Carpeting
Area Rugs and
Room Size Remnants

to blame.
around 1:45 p.m. Monday, the man left the South Trust Bank at 4095 Hancock Bridge Parkway when he grew impatient with the teller, who had to move to another unlocked drawer to get money.
About 45 minutes later, detectives believe the same man showed up at

the Pelican National Bank at 19052 S. Tamiami Trail in San Carlos. The robber approached her, he robber and told her he wanted money. She complied and the robber left with an undisclosed amount of money.
■ See ROBBERIES A3

Area couple keeps Pearl Harbor alive

BY JOAN D. LAGUARDIA
jlaguardia@news-press.com

Barney and Monica Benning are among the last of their kind, but as bombs explode in Iraq, their 63-year message remains relevant: "Remember Pearl Harbor: Keep America Alert."
On Dec. 7, 1941, 2nd Lt. Monica Conter, 27, had morning duty at Hickam Field Hospital in Oahu, Hawaii, when the Japanese attacked, destroying much of the

U.S. Pacific Fleet.
Her sweetheart, 2nd Lt. Barney Benning, camped with his unit in Barracks at military bases along Pearl Harbor over-flowed in expectation of the United States entering World War II.
The study in their independent living apartment in The Palms of Fort Myers is packed with news clippings, plaques, medals and other

■ See COUPLE A2
■ Anniversary events A2

ANDREW WEST/THE NEWS-PRESS
■ Fort Myers residents Barney and Monica Benning are the last married Pearl Harbor survivors who were in active combat.

2604

Commemorative Coins

Mrs. Benning,

Please accept the Commander's Coin on behalf of all of the men and women of the Thirteenth Air Force.

Your service to our nation has been extraordinary and will not be forgotten.

Yours Most Sincerely,

LOYD S. UTTERBACK
Lieutenant General, USAF
Commander, Thirteenth Air Force

TOM
BROKAW

·

THE
GREATEST
GENERATION
SPEAKS

·

Letters
and Reflections

To
Monica — one of
The greatest
loved you
book —

RANDOM HOUSE
NEW YORK

I Love You

THE NATIONAL

CYCLOPÆDIA OF AMERICAN

BIOGRAPHY

BEING THE

HISTORY OF THE UNITED STATES

AS ILLUSTRATED IN THE LIVES OF THE FOUNDERS, BUILDERS AND DEFENDERS
OF THE REPUBLIC, AND OF THE MEN AND WOMEN WHO ARE
DOING THE WORK AND MOLDING
THE THOUGHT OF THE
PRESENT TIME

VOLUME XLIII

New York
JAMES T. WHITE & COMPANY
1961

The National Cyclopaedia of American Biography

CONTER, Augustus Eugene, physician, was born in Baden-Baden, Germany, Apr. 21, 1871, son of John Peter and Anna (Bauer) Conter. His father was a member of the staff of the Baden-Baden casino that later moved to Monte Carlo, Monaco. After attending agricultural school in France, Augustus E. Conter came to the United States in 1889. He was graduated M.D. at the Atlanta College of Physicians and Surgeons (later Emory University) in 1902. In 1905 he took postgraduate work at the Polyclinic Hospital, New York city, and in 1915 he took a refresher course at Tulane University in New Orleans. Meanwhile, upon arriving in this country he had settled in River Junction, Fla., where he did farm

work and various odd jobs. Later he obtained employment in a Kentucky coal mine, then moved farther west, and for a time was employed at an Indian mission in Santa Fe, N.M. He returned to Florida at the outbreak of the Spanish-American War and, enlisting in the U.S. Army, served as musician with the rank of private in Company F, 3d Battalion, 1st Regiment of Infantry. After the war he returned to River Junction and was employed as attendant and handy man at Florida State Hospital, Chattahoochee, until his matriculation at medical school. On graduating, he served an internship at St. Luke's Hospital, Jacksonville, Fla. In 1903 he began a general medical practice in Madison County, Fla., and later practiced in Alachua County, Fla. About 1910, he moved his practice to Apalachicola, Fla., where, until the close of his life, he continued his professional career except for a period from 1913 to 1918, when he served as chief physician at the Florida State Hospital. While in that assignment he was responsible for the erection of the first tuberculosis hospital there. He also organized the

State Hospital Band, which was still in existence at the time of his death. Further, he served as physician for all of the major industries in the Apalachicola area. He helped establish the Franklin County Health Clinic for the Florida State Board of Health in 1936, and from 1940 until his death was medical officer at the outpatient clinic of the U.S. Public Health Service in Apalachicola. From 1909 to 1912 he served as 1st lieutenant in the Florida National Guard, in the capacity of assistant surgeon, and in the latter year was appointed a captain in the U.S. Army Medical Reserve Corps, continuing as such until 1916. Interested in civic affairs, he was a member of the district executive board of the Suwanee Council Boy Scouts of America, a charter member of the Apalachicola Rotary Club, and a member of the Apalachicola Chamber of Commerce. He belonged to the Florida State Medical Association, the American Amaryllis Society, and the Florida State Guard Rifleman's Association. A Roman Catholic in religion, he was a member of the Catholic Knights of America, Knights of Columbus, and the Holy Name Society. Politically he was an independent, having become a naturalized citizen in 1911. He was fond of music throughout his life and directed the choir at St. Patrick's Church, Apalachicola, during 1930-32. Gardening, fishing, hunting, and playing cards and chess were among his chief recreations, and art, music, languages, and photography were his special interests. Conter was married in Apalachicola, Jan. 14, 1914, to Mary Ann, daughter of Charles Lichtenfelt of that place, a merchant, and had three children: Monica Euphemia, who married Bernard Floyd Benning; Charles Augustine; and Alice Marie, who married C. Francis Jasinski. Conter died in Apalachicola, Fla., Apr. 12, 1948.

Excerpt about my father, Augustus E. Conter, M.D.
As published in The National Cyclopaedia of American Biography